THE CLOCK STRUCK ONE

A Time-Telling Tale

WRITTEN BY Trudy Harris · ILLUSTRATIONS BY Carrie Hartman

M Millbrook Press/Minneapolis

Hickory dickory dock,
      a mouse ran up the clock.

The clock struck **ONE**.
      He said, "What fun!"

(But the mouse was in for a shock.)

2

3

Hickory dickory doo, the grandfather clock struck **TWO**.

It woke the cat, who **sprang** from his mat,

hungry for mouse-tail stew.

Hickory dickory dee,
the short hand pointed to **THREE**.

"I'll search the house to find that mouse
in time for my afternoon tea."

Hickory dickory dore,
they **dashed** across the floor,

CUCKOO

8

splattering food (how terribly rude)
as the cuckoo cuckooed **FOUR**.

Hickory dickory dive,
the church bells rang out **FIVE**.

Bees entered the chase when the animals' race
tipped *over*
the honeybee hive.

Hickory dickory dix,

the clock on the

barn said **SIX**.

FEED and SEED

Park Pollard Co.

A hen joined the group when they **charged through the coop**

and frightened her new little chicks.

13

Hickory dickory deven,
a shout rang out, **"GOOD HEAVEN!**

Look at this mess.

You've ruined my dress!"

Then the clock on the oven turned **SEVEN**.

15

Hickory dickory date,
at **EIGHT**, they ran through the gate.

The farmer's son

said, "That looks *fun*.
I'm coming too. So wait!"

8:00

Hickory dickory dine, the farmer's watch said **NINE**.

He took one look, **threw** down his book,

and joined the rest in the line.

IGGY GATOR'S

MOMENT IN TIME

Hickory dickory den, they **ran** past brook and glen

20

into the town,

uphill and down,

'til the clock on the bank said **TEN**.

Hickory dickory deep,
they **staggered**, half asleep.

With a **stretch** and a yawn,
they tried to trudge on.

At **ELEVEN**,
they fell in a heap.

Hickory Dickory dell,

by **MIDNIGHT,** all was well.

With peaceful bliss,

you may think this

is all of the story to tell.

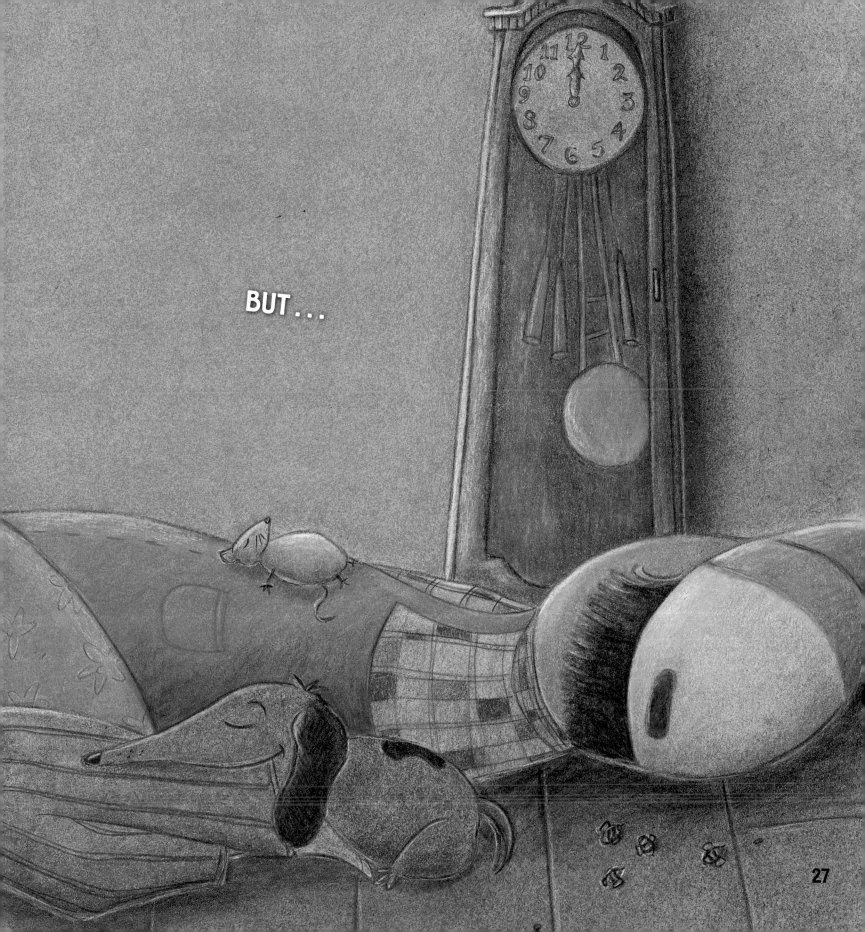

BUT . . .

Hickory dickory dun,
the grandfather clock struck **ONE!**

IT'S ABOUT TIME

Clocks tell us what time to get up in the morning, when to go to school, and even when to eat lunch. No wonder there are so many clocks in the world! Some clocks are digital. A digital clock has a time box that looks like this:

The left side of the time box tells what hour it is. The right side shows the minutes. The clock to the right shows that the hour is 1 and the minutes are 00. One hour plus zero minutes is called one o'clock.

one o'clock

It may seem strange, but time for each day actually starts in the middle of the night at midnight. Midnight is twelve o'clock A.M. One A.M. is one hour after midnight. Two hours after midnight is called two A.M. Three A.M. is three hours after midnight. Here are some pictures of how these times look on a digital clock. Can you guess what four o'clock would look like?

two o'clock   three o'clock

Some clocks are called analog (AN-uh-log) clocks. They have numbers from one to twelve printed on their "faces." These clocks also have "hands," or pointers, that move around the face. If the short hand is pointing to the number one and the long hand is pointing to twelve, the clock tells us that one hour has passed since it was twelve o'clock. The clock at the top right shows one hour and zero minutes, or one o'clock.

one o'clock

At two o'clock, the long hand points to the twelve and the short hand points to the two.

two o'clock

For three o'clock, the long hand points to the twelve and the short hand points to the three. What number do you think the short hand would point to for four o'clock?

Every hour, the long hand goes all the way around the clock and the short hand moves forward one number. The clock changes from one o'clock to two o'clock. An hour later is three o'clock, then four o'clock, five o'clock, six o'clock, seven o'clock, eight o'clock, nine o'clock, ten o'clock, eleven o'clock, and twelve o'clock. Twelve o'clock in the middle of the day is called noon, or 12 P.M. After 12 P.M., clocks start all over with one o'clock, two o'clock, and keep on going until twelve o'clock midnight comes around again.

three o'clock

This book is filled with lots of clocks, both digital and analog. How many can you find? Can you tell what time they say? Have a fun time looking!

To Christian Jones, Blake Worthington, and Thomas Liljenquist. Have a great time! Also, special thanks to my friend, Debbie Edgett. —TH

To Mrs. Rolfson, my 3rd grade teacher, thank you for encouraging me to keep drawing and creating. —CH

Text copyright © 2009 by Trudy Harris
Illustrations copyright © 2009 by Carrie Hartman

Millbrook Press
A division of Lerner Publishing Group, Inc.
241 First Avenue North
Minneapolis, MN 55401 U.S.A.

Website address: www.lernerbooks.com

Library of Congress Cataloging-in-Publication Data

Harris, Trudy.
    The clock struck one : a time-telling tale / by Trudy Harris ; illustrated by Carrie Hartman.
        p.   cm.
    Summary: Rhyming text expands on the nursery rhyme, "Hickory Dickory Dock," as a cat chases the mouse up the clock, followed by other animals, until midnight arrives and the tired creatures fall asleep. Includes facts about clocks and basic information about telling time.
    ISBN: 978-0-8225-9067-5 (lib. bdg. : alk. paper)
    [1. Clocks and watches—Fiction. 2. Time—Fiction. 3. Animals—Fiction.
4. Stories in rhyme.] I. Hartman, Carrie, ill. II. Title.
PZ8.3.H24318Clo 2009
[E]   dc22   2008041585

Manufactured in the United States of America
1 2 3 4 5 6 - JR - 14 13 12 11 10 09